I WON'T GIVE UP MY RUBBER BAND

Shinsuke Yoshitake

chronicle books · san francisco

Oh.

A rubber band.

Mommy!
Mommy!

Are you throwing
away this rubber band?!

Yay!
I have a rubber band!

This is *my* rubber band!

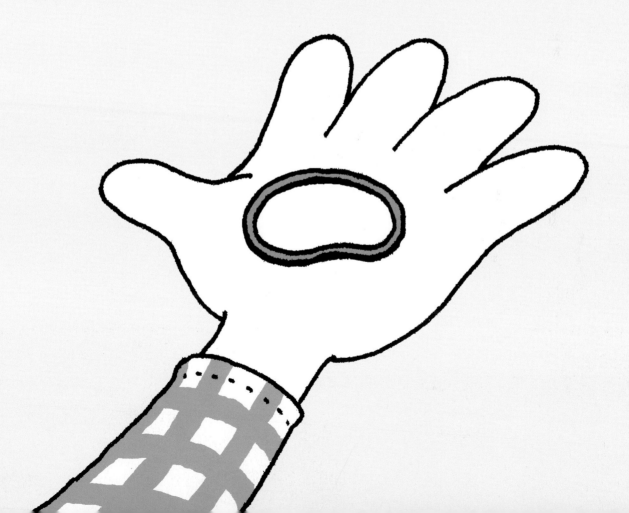

I have always wanted
something that was just mine.

Not my brother's hand-me-down . . .

Not something that
I had to share . . .

Not something that
I could only borrow
for a little while . . .

My mom let me have this rubber band.
It is mine.

And I can do anything I want with it!
Isn't that great?

This rubber band is for just me
to use and not for anyone else!

Today we'll take a bath together.

And, of course, we'll sleep in the same bed.

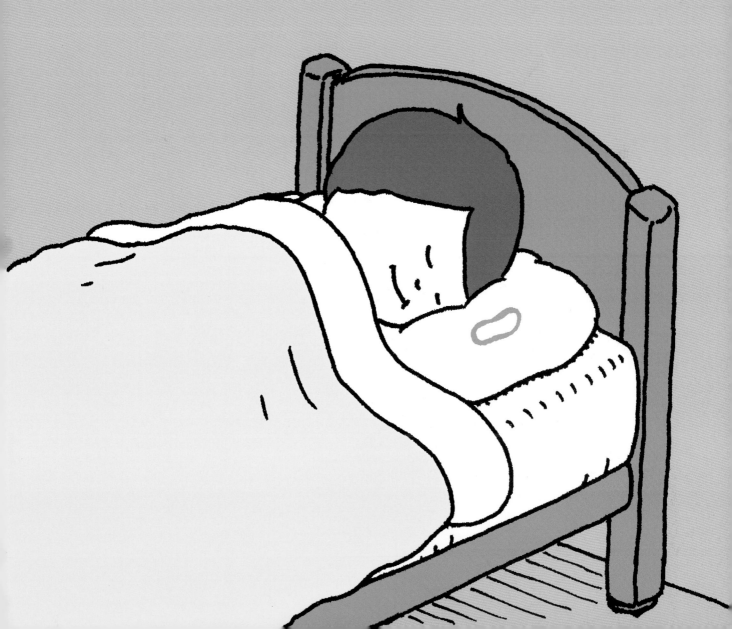

When I grow up, I'll wear this rubber band as fashion.

I'll bundle up all the
love letters I receive
with this rubber band.

And I might catch all the bad people in the world with this rubber band.

When the time comes, I will save the
world with this rubber band.

I won't give it to anyone.
It is *my* treasure, after all.

Of course, one day, when I meet my soul mate . . .

I might let him tie his rubber band to mine.

My brother will definitely
laugh at my rubber band.

That's all right.
I don't think he's ready to understand it.

It's not as if I really understand
my brother's things, either.

But I don't make fun of his treasures.

Now that I think about it,
my next-door neighbor Nori
was holding onto a lid all day.

And Takumi has a ring that
he found on the street.

Grandma always wears the watch that Grandpa gave her.

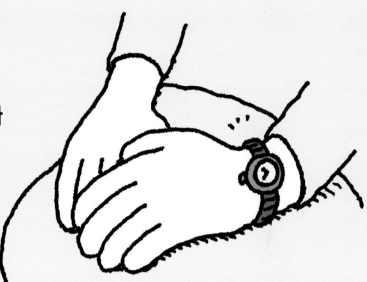

Daddy takes really good care of his old model car.

It seems like everyone wants to
keep their treasures for themselves.

That's why everyone always seems to be looking for something.

As long as I have this rubber band,
I'll be okay, even if I hurt my arm.

I can even exercise.

With this rubber band . . .

Ready . . .

My rubber band and I will visit animals all over the world.

Poing

Poing

Swish

And then we'll play with them.

If I buy lots of presents, I can bring them home with my rubber band!

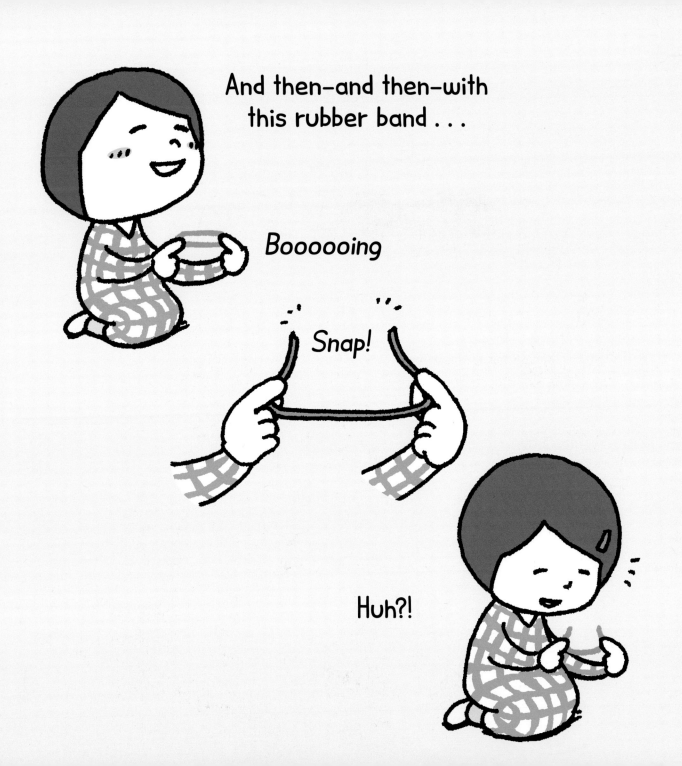

Oh?

Ohhhh . . .

It broke . . .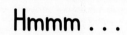

Shuffle, shuffle
Rustle, rustle

Rustle, rustle
Rustle . . .

Mommy!

Mommy!

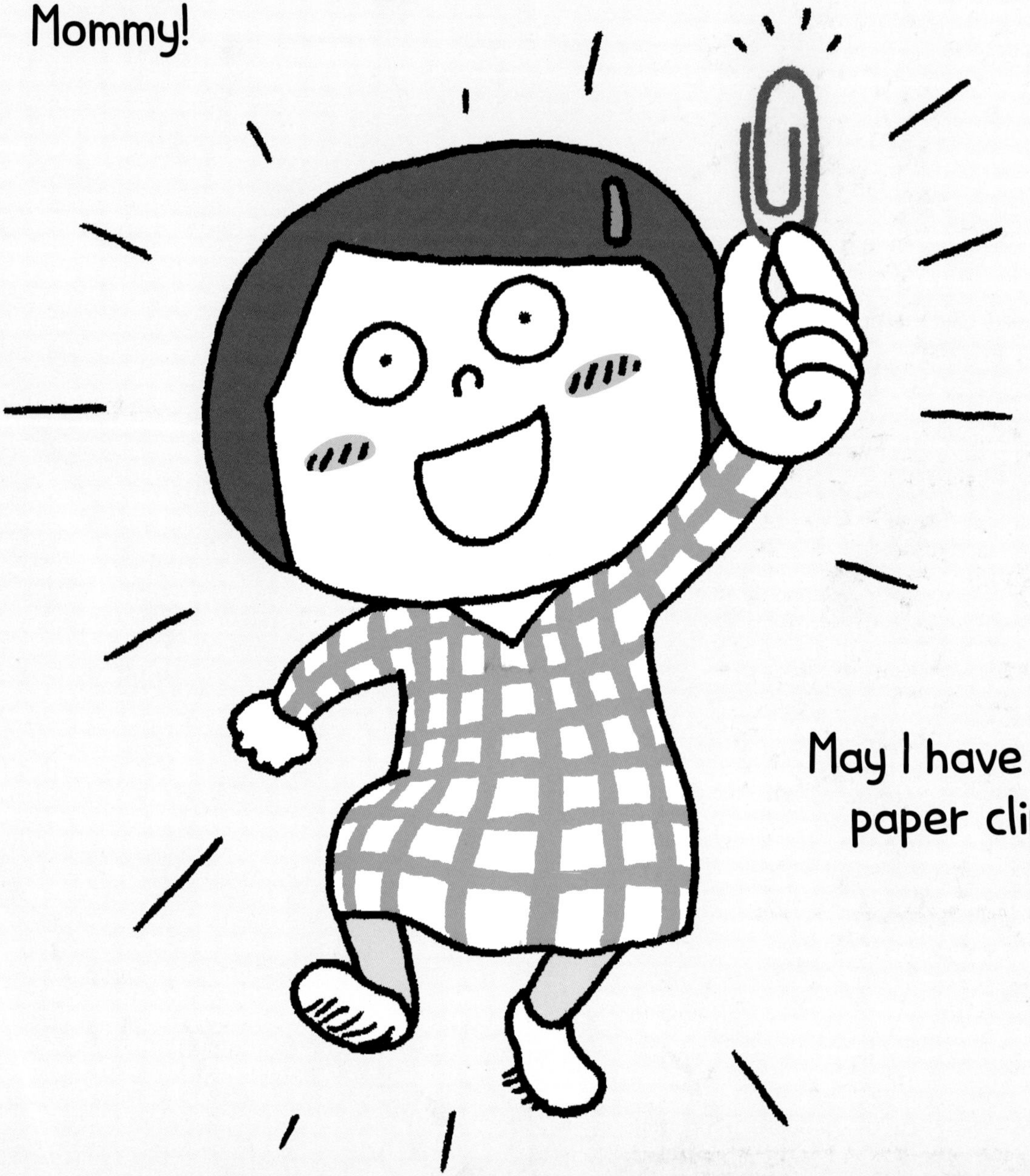

May I have this paper clip?